I0605001

# Heavy Mettle: Heresy

## The birth of a vampyre

<u>**Books by Lewis King**</u>

<u>Keyholder Series</u>
The Beautiful Man Without Mercy

<u>Heavy Mettle Series</u>
Heresy

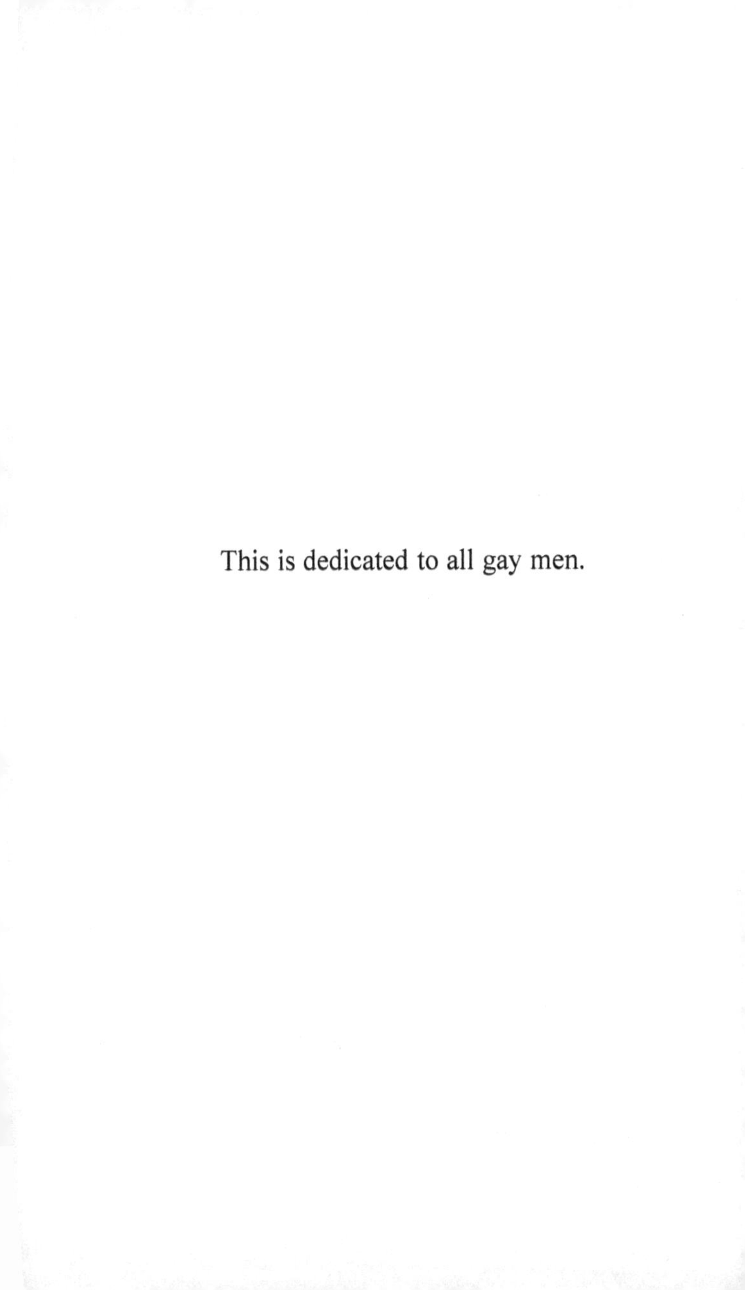

This is dedicated to all gay men.

# I

"Out. Get OUT! You ruined it!."

Haytham was hurried out of the man's front door just in time to get his trousers back on. Otherwise, his crumpled shirt and dirty boots were all clutched in his arms as he stood in the cold, morning street shirtless and barefoot.

It wasn't a private scene either. Haytham started to turn red and hide his chest behind his clothes as he noticed the early risers around them stopping to stare. There were farmers with crates of produce on their way to market and members of the city guard changing for the next day's shift.

"It wasn't that bad," he tried to say in a calm voice, "it was an accident!"

"You told me you loved me," the man in the doorway hissed. Haytham couldn't help but notice that he'd taken the time to dress before starting this little scene. "You don't even know my last name."

Haytham rolled his eyes, "therefore you know I didn't mean it like that. It was a compliment! You just felt that good it kinda... came out." He smiled nervously hoping to diffuse the situation, at least long enough to come back in and put his shoes on.

"Go!" was all he earned from his now ex-lover.

Depressed, Haytham slinked away into the alleyway nearby where he could finally tighten his breeches properly. As he left, any onlookers went about their day pretending to have seen nothing. He knew he would be hearing about the encounter for at least the next week, however. Between housewives with their hushed gossiping as they hang the clothes out and the way men talk over beers – it would be citywide news by nightfall!

He huffed, already doing his best to let it go, as he emerged from the other side of the alley fully dressed now.

He made his way back home along the cobbles of his humble town. Havendon may have been the capital city but Dunmere, the borough where Haytham lived, was on the outskirts by fields and farms. His own house, even, stood on the forest line just past the end of the road. There he lived in seclusion, his only guests tending to be those on their way to and from a hunt.

It was one of the few sights that still managed to make him smile at least. He rarely got business, being known as a dark mage and all, but it still made him proud to see the sign of his shop above his door each day.

Even if the circumstances he saw it in tended to be during the walk of shame back home in the mornings.

After all, the tizzy he found himself in that day was just one at the end of a long line of many, many disappointed men. For some unexplainable reason, Haytham just couldn't keep a guy on his arm.

Which lead him to make a very questionable judgement when he moved to rest on his bed at last. He was tired of rejection and matted with sweat when he rolled his head over the pillow and happened to spy a tome he acquired a few years ago from some dusty, travelling salesman.

The Enchiridion Daemonia.

No author was credited – and the title wasn't really anything more than overdramatic flare – but it was an encyclopaedia for summoning various daemons. Haytham had bought it just in case he needed it despite never really being a strong member of any religion.

He had initially left it in his library but a year ago, when a man refused his eager proposal, he had pondered finding a solution in those pages. He talked himself out of it of course but he still left the volume by his bedside.

Just in case.

Again, about six months ago, he had flicked through the pages and found one that showed Archdaemon Loxas, lord of men (meaning, males.) This was when he had sorely misinterpreted the rapport he had going with a handsome customer who, as it turned out, was not even interested in males, as it were.

But still, he talked himself out of it then as well, rationalising that if it didn't happen naturally, love probably wasn't worth it.

He did leave that page earmarked, however.

Just in case.

Now though, sick of the organic approach, the dark mage had made his decision to once and for all commit to these just-in-cases he had been setting aside.

He sat up straight and grabbed the book. It's cover was the deep blue of the night sky and lined in gold decorations. It was large and heavy and leatherbound. It's pages were yellowed with age but surprisingly not fragile.

He decided the best place to perform a ritual of any kind was most likely the basement. He shuffled, still in his sweat ridden clothes, out of his room. The house – that doubled as his shop – was not the biggest. There was an attic on the first floor then there was the ground floor with the living room transformed into a shopfront. It had a counter and all manner of shelves covered in various arcane goods. In the back was a small kitchen, bathroom and then his bedroom: just as cramped. Down in the basement was where he had an open room. In the early, ambitious days of his business, he had kept crates of wares and goods he had intended to sell. Nowadays he only kept a more... direct inventory.

This just left a cold, grey and slightly damp cellar with three or four crates huddled in a corner.

He took a moment, bringing his broom from upstairs, to give a quick sweep over the floor and brush at any cobwebs but the room still screamed dingy whether he liked it or not.

Maybe the daemon would be more comfortable in scuff?

It doesn't matter; he needed this. He wanted this.

He sat in the centre of the room cross legged, the book open in his lap, and read the words in his mind. He held his palms out and closed his eyes, repeating the words in his mind again and again. As the thought, the intent, rippled through his body and tapped into his magical potency, he could begin to feel the room around him shift.

The torches hung in rusted brackets all blew out one by one as a wind coursed through the space. Haytham shivered at the vortex but carried on none the less.

Soon the walls started to ripple as if made of liquid, their colours shifting between a miasma of crimson reds. The torches began to relight, now with cold, icy blue flames instead. The glow and the walls cast the wind in a deep purple that filled Haytham's vision as he opened his eyes once more to bear witness to his actions.

Regret started to fill him but he was too far beyond the point of it now that he had no choice but to reach his hand out to the air before him. As he moved, straining hard to push against the wind, a limb began to emerge from the wall. It was a large, muscled arm stretching out from the sea of his shifting walls. It clawed forward and further until at last the two men's hands met in the middle and embraced.

As the fingers intertwined, suddenly the chaos surrounding him stopped. There was a blink – a flash – as Haytham pulled on the arm and brought it from the land of hellfire and torment and into the world of the living once more.

The fruits of his efforts stood before him: a daemon at seven feet tall. His skin was dark red and his hair midnight black. It covered his head in a mess of curls and also decorated his chest, arms and legs. The black hair dusted his chin and armpits too while also trailing down from his naval and leading teasingly to a brown loincloth that hung very low at his hips.

"Up here," he commanded, tilting Haytham's head up with the tip of one pointed finger nail.

Loxas didn't seem too impressed by the ogling and once the human had finally managed to settle his eye contact he grinned a lopsided smile.

"You're looking good, Ysard. What's it been, ten years?" his voice was deep and smooth. It was the kind of voice that compelled Haytham to bark 'yes sir!' no matter what it said.

He managed to control himself though and finally answer, "um, Ysard? Do you mean that old king of Yorrick?"

The beast blinked, "not... him then?"

"Not for two hundred years, no."

"Yikes. It has been a while since he wrote that little book of his."

Haytham pondered the historical implications of learning the author of this daemon book but decided to put that away for another day. He shook his head and said, "look, that doesn't matter. I brought you here to ask a favour-"

"A FAVOUR?" the daemon boomed. As he did, the now restored orange fires on the wall erupted with his anger. "No angelic ring to protect you and no safety around your place of summoning," he held his arms out grandiosely to indicate the space, "yet, young man-"

"I'm twenty-six."

"You dare to implore a favour of ME?"

The beast took a deep breath. As he did, the fires seemed to calm to their natural flames. He pushed back locks of hair that had fallen in his face and then stood back up straight, Haytham still sat pathetically on the floor in front of him.

"What do you want then, eh? Love is it?"

Haytham nodded meekly. "Lord of men, I wanted you to bring me my... my soulmate. I'm sick of searching- ah!"

Loxas wrapped his hand around the air, a chain appearing between his fingers with the movement. The chain snaked from his grip down to attach to a collar that had appeared in flames around the magician's neck. He pulled, thrusting the man to his feet – to his tiptoes – so that he could nearly, but not quite, be close to his level.

"If that is what your heart desires..." the daemon cooed. Haytham was grasping tightly to loosen the collar around his neck while Loxas ignored him and continued the show. He held up a long index finger that ended in a pointed, black finger nail and swirled it gently in the air between them. As he did, like candy floss, two whisps began to swirl and collect around the point. There was a red wind and a blue one, both dancing but not yet mixing. Haytham realised what they were with wide eyes; a living soul and an infernal one.

"I can bind us, hm? Unite our souls and we can live together on this earth as one another's kings."

"Yes." Haytham replied flatly.

Loxas was surprised. He blinked and stared at the man before him, truly in disbelief that the man had said that not just quickly but so assuredly.

He was meant to be the one doing the bluffing, the scaring, the intimidation! Yet here he was, looking at this desperate soul and feeling like it was he at whim to the deal.

"You want to merge your soul with a daemon's? Forever?"

Haytham nodded, his eyes wide and yearning. "At first I thought I wanted a soulmate. Then I saw you and thought I might just want you to fuck me, like that would sort me out. But now... well... I've heard the stories of the grace of angels and wickedness of red devils and all I can say, after seeing you, is that you're the one with grace." He swallowed nervously, struggling against the collar, but carried on eagerly still. "The black hair and red skin is a consequence of a life lived how you chose – it's a punishment inflicted on yourself for living and loving and loving living. And angels beauty just comes from being perfect. What could be more boring?"

Loxas was stunned for a moment, processing this human's confession.

"And what, pray tell," he finally managed to stammer out, "do I enjoy from this arrangement?"

Words left Haytham now. He had nothing. He was nothing but desperate. All he knew was that he wanted Loxas, to feel his warm embrace and to get to know every inch of his sin in life and death. He knew this was it, this was him and them and everything! More than love at first sight, a match struck in his own decision – soulmates by design. What could be more alluring?

So, resolute, he at last managed to give the daemon his answer. He raised a hand to tangle in the stretches of black hair on the back of Loxas' neck and pulled him down into a deep and passionate kiss.

# II

Loxas leant into his kiss, pinning the man against the cold, stone wall.

As they made out – their tongues dancing together in hot, sticky breaths – Haytham experienced a dichotomy of sensation completely new to him.

Where his back ground against the wall, even through his shirt, he felt rough, grating cold. But his wrists, pinned by Loxas' iron grip, were starting to feel blisteringly hot.

The collar had gone now but the tears still brimmed at his eyes and fell down his face from the overwhelming feeling of being on the edge of both too hot and too cold.

It wasn't until after five minutes of gratuitously moaning into the daemon's mouth that he realised the pair were completely naked.

*Infernal magic* he thought to himself as he turned his attention to the mischievous glimmer in Loxas' eyes. The strangest feeling amongst all these senses however was the unashamedness. He wasn't trying to close his legs – the daemon nestled firmly between his thighs now – but instead he was actively spreading them wider so desperate to be touched there.

His desire, his need to feel this man, trumped any feelings of embarrassment as he decided he would sooner get on his knees and beg then let this man leave without feeling every pleasure of his infernal body.

The tongue sucking stopped then as Haytham suddenly lost control of himself for a moment, his eyes rolling back in the sudden pleasure of Loxas rubbing their members together. The mage was average sized, no one had called him big nor small, but the daemon, surprisingly, wasn't that much bigger. Eight inches, maybe, of thick, red muscle. It was shrouded at the base by neatly trimmed, black hair and came to end at a purple head that revealed itself with each thrust. When that moment came of Loxas' grinding up, where both their sensitive, leaking tips were exposed, Haytham would grunt and do his best to revel in that moment of ecstasy before the daemon pulled back again. Soon his own hips were moving involuntarily to rub harder against his newest partner's body.

"Fu-huh-huckkk," he managed to spill some words out at last, driven crazy by the near-climaxes of each grind. "Ride me please, ride me now!" he begged.

The daemon chuckled. "Hey now, handsome man, let's not be too hasty." As his words teased out, Loxas' tail began to wind and curl up the inner thigh of his human consort. It was a thin appendage that ended in a triangular tip. It sprouted from his muscled back just above his ass. It seemed to stretch to be as long as it needed to for Loxas' purposes, whatever they may be.

Right now that purpose was pushing a particularly needy mage over the edge. That soft tringle end moved further up to tease and nestle underneath Haytham's balls. With that first slight touch, the man let out a squeak that turned into some sort of animal groaning as he audibly begged for more without using any words at all.

The tail continued to wrap around and tickle at the sensitive areas around and below his cock, maintaining a constant edge of climax that caused Haytham's legs to start shaking and shuddering.

"You can cum just from this, yes?" he cooed as the still pinned man gritted his teeth in frustration.

"Puh-please!" he breathed, his head leaning forward hungry to taste the daemon again. Loxas obliged and restarted the dance of tongues between their mouths. As they went on, their breath's started to change colour, taking on that wispy complexion of the devil's earlier illusion.

Loxas' heavy, red breathing mixed with the sticky, deep blues of Haytham's. The air around them turned into a sparkle of hot, royal purple as the two men became bound to one another.

"Here's the deal," Loxas proposed, his own voice shuddering now as his thrusts pulled him near climax too, "I will be your loving boyfriend till the day you die and in return I get to play with you whenever I want. How does that sound?" It took a few seconds for Haytham to register those words.

1 – Loxas' voice was so seductive that for a moment it simply blended in with the harmony of other sensations that Haytham was experiencing.

2 – He had to focus to realise that 'play with you' meant 'fuck you.' Okay, that's being kind. The daemon wanted to rape him as he pleased.

And Haytham's response to that?

He moved his hands, Loxas letting his wrists free, to grip tightly onto the sides of the beast's heads. He pushed their foreheads together and looked him deep in the eyes so he could say, ostensibly clearly, "I would kill every one of God's creations if it gave me the privilege of being even your slave."

Loxas responded with violent exuberance. He slammed Haytham back against the wall, pinning him harder now, and moved in to ravage his new toy. He sat himself on the sensitive cock of the human and rode him to orgasm countless times, using a spell of some sort to keep him in a state of arousal. He pushed his tail into his hole to stimulate that special spot and send his seed rushing inside him time after time. And he gnawed at that soft, supple, human neck until it gushed with blood only to lick it with a magical tongue that flawlessly fixed the wound. When all was done, Haytham – after falling in and out of blissful unconsciousness – had decided that that part was his favourite. The breaking of skin hurt like hell but the repairing with his hot, daemon tongue was akin to the pleasure on his prostate tenfold.

In the following daze of carrying himself upstairs and washing in the cold water of his measly wooden basin, Haytham slowly processed all that went down in the basement. Most importantly, he recapped himself on the deal he had signed on for.

He was unsure about it as he dried himself and dressed; worried that he had ruined his life by living at the end of a daemon's leash. But when he went back into his bedroom and saw the tall red devil laying there on his sheets he couldn't help but smile.

It was time for him to do his part.

His new boyfriend.

And he did it well, laying there with his arms open, Haytham came and wound down from the overstimulation of their play by wrapping his arms around Loxas and nuzzling into his arms. His nose tickled against the black hair of his pits and he was soothed by the subtle scent of musk.

His final anxiety came alongside the realisation that Loxas probably wasn't enjoying this part like he was. He suddenly felt a bit of hollowness amidst his reverie as he clued into the delusion of it all – his new one sided love.

But when he looked up at him he was reminded of that fact that whether the daemon had wanted love before or not didn't matter – for he was smiling.

For their souls were now united till death does them part.

# III

Their bliss only continued after that.

Haytham was so grateful every day that he had a man now who would not only listen to his latest mystical ramblings about some book or orb or stave or what not but who also actually understood him.

While 'lord of men' usually left his powers more in the realm of the bedroom, he still had a knowledge of ages. It provided very useful for their eternal back and forths on some topic of magic or another. Discussions that went on all day and all night until Haytham would finally collapse from fatigue in the arms of his love.

Of course, Loxas' benefit was still held up. He would take his partner whenever his cock got hard and as Haytham quickly learned that didn't happen with care for what he was doing.

There were many complaints of 'I'm working!' that were usually silenced by a sudden mouthful of daemon. There were baths that had to take twice as long due to Loxas catching him in the water and making him all dirty again. At least he could heat water for him with his infernal body though.

The worst was in the middle of the night when Haytham found himself suddenly lurched into the land of the awake by a pointed tail pressing against any number of sensitive body parts.

'You can cum just from this,' had also become the Daemon's new favourite game as he would rub against a hard nipple or grind against a begging hole until the mindfuck climaxed his human.

But the most annoying part? The aspect of it all that really ground into Haytham after every one of these indulgent sessions?

He always loved it.

No matter what his arguments are at the start the daemon would always do exactly what it took to have him begging for more by the end. 'Lord of men' turned out to be a gross understatement as

Loxas consistently managed to play his body like an instrument.

Despite it all though, Haytham never found regret in his relationship. He may still be just as financially ruined as he always had been but that suddenly stopped feeling like a problem whenever he got to fall asleep on the pillows of his boyfriend's chest.

Across the past two weeks of slow work, sad meals and general infamy around town, Haytham had been happiest he had ever been.

He even bothered to start dressing nice again. He had always had a couple of outfits he'd either inherited from family or found in an abandoned settlement that he looted but it was the maintaining them that prevented his wearing them. So while in the past he may have simply walked around in some scuffed up, black trousers, a wrinkled white shirt and some worn, leather boots; he now wore exactly the same thing except with a nice, royal blue coat over the top.

"It makes you look more magical," Loxas said, using the heat from his steaming skin to iron out a few of the folds in it.

"What does that even mean?" Haytham asked, brushing his fingers back through his soft, brown hair. It was a mess on his head that he tamed only by combing with his fingers.

The two had been sat at the front desk of his shop all day just in case a customer came to ask of his services despite the fact that the door had a bell.

"It's just... colourful. It makes sense, trust me," the daemon said kissing him on the cheek. "Maybe now that you have your new outfit..."

"*No*," the human groaned. "I'm a dark mage and that's that."

"All I'm saying is that there are much more, uh, respectful... professional! Titles out there."

Haytham scoffed, "you're just worried about your reputation. Tell me, has anyone other than me and a king summoned you?"

"Only once," he said grinning. He stalked over to stand behind his partner where he slid a hand around and up his neck to tilt his head back. "Besides, you're a king to me."

Haytham blushed and smiled, "I didn't feel like royalty last time we were in this position," he mumbled, his neck straining.

"You're right. Kings aren't normally the ones getting their mouth's spat in-"

The doorbell rang.

Loxas disappeared in a puff of steam and Haytham wobbled to rebalance himself on the stall.

The pair had agreed that the whole daemon boyfriend aspect was best left a secret as not to completely deter potential customers.

This particular customer, however, couldn't seem to be impressed no matter what. Just as Haytham managed to sit back up straight on his stool, an old woman with greyed hair and a faded pink shawl strode inside looking about herself to make sure she wasn't observed.

She even continued to look left and right, analysing and scrutinising, as she walked over to desk.

"Are you the dark whats-his-name that helps with magic and the like," she whispered, leaning in close. She never looked directly at him, her eyes always wondering to her peripheral vision.

"Yes, I'm the..." an idea came to mind then, spurred by his previous conversation, "I'm the warlock around here!" He stood up, hands proudly on his lapel. "What can I do you for?"

The old lady looked to be regretting the encounter already.

"Stupid young man," she hissed under her breath, "look here," she snapped her finger, "all I want is fire. That's all, if you please."

"Fire," he repeated. "You want fire."

"Yes you simpleton, FIRE!"

He pulled away from her, concerned.

"Is this fire for anything in particular?"

"Mould."

Haytham waited for her to elaborate but she just stared impatiently back at him, her eyes slowly widening.

He cleared his throat, "right well that's a bit extreme. What kind of mould are we talking about?"

"Chicken."

"*Chicken.*"

She just stared back, confused as to why he kept repeating her words. He scoured his mind to try and think what she could possibly mean but came up with nothing.

"Why don't you show me, do you live near?"

"I'm not telling you my address!"

"Just take me to yours and I'll deal with it personally. No extra charge, eh?"

She pondered this, sucking at her gums for a few uncomfortable seconds before nodding.

"Fine."

"Amazing. Just wait a mo' while I grab some supplies then I'll be with you right away!" As he walked off to the cellar he started to mentally kick himself for his over enthusiastic customer service impression.

"I thought it was cute." When he reached the bottom of the stairs he saw Loxas there waiting for him, the torches already lit.

The human just sighed, trying his best to forget about it, "hey, I've got to go out for a bit for some work, but I should be home soon." As he spoke he had been rummaging around in some of those wooden crates in the corner, filling his inside pockets with various wands and stones in case he might need any of it to deal with whatever this mould was.

As he moved back towards the staircase, the daemon suddenly grabbed his wrist and pulled him back.

"Oh really not now, I need to-"

Loxas smirked, "human boy, what if I wanted you?"

Haytham swallowed nervously knowing that there was nothing he could do to stop him. "Please," he groaned.

Loxas gripped tighter and hotter on his wrist, scaring Haytham, before suddenly letting go with a laugh.

"Ha, just winding you up."

Haytham chuckled nervously as his boyfriend kissed him on the cheek.

"But remember," the daemon whispered in his ear, "if I wanted to I could. Whenever. *Wherever.*"

Haytham left quickly, knowing that his palpable fear was exactly what the red devil had wanted.

This whole time of no work and laying about at home had left him feeling like there was really little downside to their arrangement. But with that rare chance of work at his door, he was starting to realise, for the first time in all this mad endeavour, that maybe he had taken far too big a risk.

# IV

"*Chicken of the woods*," he corrected sternly.

The lady harumphed her indifference.

The warlock had come to her house, not far down their unnamed street, to inspect this mould only to find that there were shelves of fungus growing from her wall.

It was a quaint cottage with a nice, albeit dusty, front room. On one of the slightly peeling walls was a large, black patch of what was clearly some sort of mould. It swirled at the edges with uncomfortably soft greys.

But that could only be seen on the edges for the entire spot was sprouting red, yellow and orange shelves of mushroom. Thick and warped, they stuck out like an eyesore.

When Haytham went over to touch it, slowly holding his fingers out, the lady commented again, "I wouldn't touch that if I were you."

He did anyway brushing his fingertips across the ridges of the growth.

"Have you?" he asked, "touched it?"

"No," she replied scornfully, "I just said that I wouldn't. Fucking idiot."

"Pardon?" he politely pretended not to hear that last part.

"Nothing, deary. Now are you getting rid of it or what?"

He pulled his hand away, deciding that there was nothing abnormal about it at all. Mould and spores. "Yeah, yeah. It just seems like it got out of control is all-"

"OUT OF CONTROL?" she huffed, "it wasn't there last night, I tell you. I wake up to see this abomination on my wall and suddenly I'm letting my house, *my homestead,* get out of control?"

"Alright, alright," he tried to calm her down but had to settle for moving on swiftly. Still, he was curious. All this overnight? He moved over to it and pulled a silver athame from a sheath inside his coat. He sawed off one of the ridges and tucked it away into his coat for later analysis.

He then took a safe step backwards, inhaled and held his right hand out towards the mould. He pointed the palm at the left edge of it and, as he cast his magic, moved his hand with a slow but heavy exertion over the length of the shelves.

As he went, a small, controlled flame ate away at the fungus. It didn't spread or consume it simply nipped along the path that Haytham drew with his hand and disappeared as he moved away.

As it went, even the black on the wall behind was burned off. By the time he was done the wall was completely cleared of the strange infection. When he lowered his hand he finally exhaled then took a moment to catch his breath again.

He shook out his arm to stretch away the exertion and then turned to his customer with a satisfied grin.

"That should be you all sorted, ma'am," he held his hand out to her. "I implore you to get in contact again if it reappears."

She shook her head, annoyed, as she pulled a couple of silver coins out to cross his palm, "why, so you can fleece me again?" After she made her payment she stood aside and threw a pointed finger to the front door, "I'm sure you'd love that wouldn't you. Go on you cheeky beggar, out."

He just nodded his thanks as he showed himself out of the building.

The mushroom still lurked in his mind though and the sample weighed heavy in his jacket. As he walked on down that unnamed street of his, he decided to stop at three other houses to ask after any similar issues.

Each old person that opened the door told him no in about as many words as 'go away.' He had chosen to open up his shop here thinking that he could be of help to the oft-neglected elderly community of the borough. He failed to factor in that these conservative types tended to naturally reject warlocks.

So after that fourth and final home he decided to give up deigning to return to Loxas – no doubt the man was eagerly waiting to have him.

"Excuse me. Sir!" Haytham stopped in his tracks to heed a masculine voice behind him. He turned to see a tall man in white robes waving a hand of hello.

The warlock looked around to see where he could have come from; he was familiar with all his neighbours and this part of the town tended to be rather sheltered. It was truly strange then that he hadn't an inkling of where this person appeared from.

The only thing stranger however was his dress. He was tall, six five, and wearing a set of white robes that were astonishing for quite how white they were – i.e. very clean.

He was blond as well with brown eyes. An unusual pairing in these parts.

"Can I help you?" Haytham asked, a little uncomfortable.

"Yes, yes you can!" he smiled, "I've been tracing some dark, dark forces indeed. It all seems to centre around here – or rather – around you." The bright man smiled but that did not make his words any less rude, "you wouldn't happen to know anything about that, would you?"

Haytham blinked a few times as he swallowed the man's request. Then a thought, at last, came to mind. "Oh, uh, it might be this you're looking for." He rustled his hand around inside his coat until he found the sawed off shelf of mushroom. He held it out to show the man but he winced and reeled away.

"Yikes!" he held his hands up, "yes, that would do it! Thank you for your help mister, I'll be away now."

"Wait, do you know what this is? Help me, help us!" he implored.

But the man was no longer there. He hadn't disappeared in a sparkle or a puff of smoke he just stopped being there where once he was.

Haytham blinked and rubbed his eyes, the sudden lack of something where once a man stood was messing with his brain.

When he finally caught up to it, though, and a few puzzles pieces finally fell into place, he asked himself a very strange but important question.

*Was that an angel?*

# V

Haytham kept denying it but that didn't stop Loxas from asking again and again.

The warlock had been too nervous, too afraid, to bring up his heavenly encounter with his infernal boyfriend so it left the pair in a lot of awkward silences. Haytham tried his best to act normal but the only thing rushing through his mind a lot of the time was *'don't talk about heaven, don't talk about heaven.'*

Soon the whether-he-liked-it-or-not sex was the easier part of his life as it was the only time he truly couldn't keep his mind on anything other than how much he loved his great, big daemon boyfriend.

He had also been nipping out for 'work' a lot the past week. Not just to escape the wondering glare of his concerned partner but also to ask around about the strange mould.

An angel shying away from it made him feel, in his guts, like something was very wrong. He had mandated his own sort of patrol to resolve this where he would go to a new section of town every day and knock on all the doors to see if anyone had seen anything similar.

Just like every prior attempt, however, no one had seen anything.

Apparently.

He knew very easily that a lot of people were lying to him. Not just the people on his street but the young, the workers – everyone! The common man's attitude to the warlock was a cynical one, no less a warlock known for his embarrassing social life.

After his final house of the day he trotted solemnly over to the nearest well, shoved his face in the deep hole, and cursed.

"Shitting, shitting, shit, shit, shit, fuck, *shit*!"

The shouts reverberated against the water and echoed back up but it was starting to be dusk by then so he was thankfully alone.

With his anger shouted out, he calmed down and looked at his reflection in the water below. As he stopped panting and the water stopped shaking he saw a very desperate man indeed looking back.

"Oh shit," he grunted finally as he realised that he needed Loxas.

He needed to confide in him, not to get more information but just to find some comfort. The angel had only stressed himself out and while he had told himself that his active search for the mould was helping it was truthfully only amplifying that anxiety.

If people needed help, if people *wanted* help, they would come to him.

Just like he should have come to Loxas a long time ago.

*     *     *

Haytham eased his way into the conversation.

When he had come home, and Loxas was surprised to see his human initiating for once, he had meant it when he said he was simply craving him.

He had forgotten quite how big his daemon was though, as when he removed those shaggy, brown trousers (that he had finally convinced him to wear instead of just a loincloth) he only unearthed a very thick appendage. He remembered that the length was nothing too astonishing but the girth was hard to handle. As was the heat of his eye watering seed.

Haytham still powered on like a good boy though.

He even enjoyed watching the way Loxas would revel with each of his gags and chokes.

*'I'm such a good boyfriend,'* he thought to himself proudly after finishing the daemon off and wiping away any leaking semen from his chin.

"D'you not want me to finish you off?" Loxas asked as Haytham immediately moved on to the snuggling part of their sessions.

"I'm alright. That's all I needed, honest."

Loxas just shrugged, happy to have helped.

*'I'm such a good boyfriend,'* he also thought to himself.

The two let themselves lay there, satisfied, for a while. Both were nude and comfortable being entangled together and warm. It was soft and supple and sweet.

Haytham even found himself starting to drift off before snapping himself awake again when he remembered his goal in all this.

"Tired?" the daemon asked as he noticed the nodding off.

The warlock nodded lazily but didn't let his eyes close again.

"I've actually been wondering something for a while..." he said, braving the conversation at last.

"Uh huh?"

He didn't dare to outright ask about his angelic encounter so he started to broach the subject by treading lightly.

"I just wanted to ask if you knew what heaven was like. I mean, I'd like to know what I'm missing out on."

Loxas snickered. "And you think a daemon is the best person to ask about that?"

"Right, I suppose I hadn't thought of that." He faltered, anxious to think of a new way to attack the matter until he noticed his boyfriend chuckling.

"Nah, I know what heaven's like. They taunt us about it down there. Show us what we could have won."

"Wow," Haytham breathed, "that's quite-"

"If you're about to point out that actual hell is mean then I have some news for you."

"Alright, dickhead. Are you going to tell me what heaven's like or not?"

The daemon sat up on the bed into a more comfortable position as he deliberated on how exactly was best to describe it. Haytham lay next to him with his head in his lap. He looked up at Loxas with yearning eyes.

Heaven itself was less a place and more an idea. What Loxas was struggling to do was put that idea into words. At last he decided on one aspect of that infinite idea that he thought best encapsulated the afterlife.

"When people go to heaven they don't become angels at the same age they died. They become angels at the age they were happiest at in life. That's why when you see all these marble statues or illustrious paintings, most of the angels are depicted as children or babies. Because the way it tends to be is that those who genuinely lived their life in service to God's laws and earn their way into paradise were only ever really happy when they were kids. Childhood is the only time they enjoyed."

Haytham stared up at him still, his eyes now in awe instead of yearning. He got it now. He knew he might have been damned a long time ago – definitely now with his choice of lover – but this new take on the afterlife had cemented his contentedness.

"You know," he replied breathlessly, "I think being an adult is the only time I've felt joy. I can indulge, I can choose, I can be."

Loxas grins, "you can play with your cock whenever you want."

Haytham elbowed him in the stomach and sat up ignoring the daemon's grunt. "Not just that!"

"I know, I know," he says, leaning over to kiss his man on the forehead. "I'm sorry."

Haytham couldn't stop himself from smiling and that brought his boyfriend's smile on as well.

In the end, the two went back to their cuddling, this time in happy, peaceful silence rather than strangeness.

For Haytham the air had been cleared, at least keeping his anxieties at bay for a while now.

For Loxas however... well he knew that that question had not come from nowhere. Between the warlock's sudden interest in taking his work outside, the patches of awkwardness that had been passing between them recently and now this odd questioning, the daemon had no doubt that something was up.

He let them both fall asleep together for now but he was resolute in worming the truth from him tomorrow.

# VI

Haytham decided to keep on with his little excursions. Previously, he had been lying to Loxas by telling him that his trips out to ask for the mould were actually efforts of self-promotion; that he was pushing the business.

Today he thought to actually give that a go.

"Haytham Rayne, your local warlock, is here to help!" he said with a cheery smile. He was stood beside farmers, tanners, butchers and tailors at the marketplace in town yelling out to promote his services as much as everyone else.

He had no stall yet but he had brought along a couple of mystical appliances, tomes and artifacts to show off. He caught the attention of some kids out with their mother by waving a shiny crystal. Some inquisitive governess had stopped by, unable to resist asking about the different books he was showing off. He even managed to hand his address out to a prospective customer – a middle-aged man with a hush-hush need to improve his work in the bedroom.

"I fear the missus 'as been eyeing up the blacksmith as of recently," he gulped after his harsh whispering. The warlock replied in an equal measure of quiet,

"worry not, sir. I have a spell that can make you last longer and harder than the blacksmith could even dream of." He winked as the man nodded quietly back.

While these three were his only aproachees, he still counted the day as a great success. He had probably drummed up more business in those five hours of standing and yelling than in the past five years of being the resident magician.

As lunchtime came around and the sun nestled comfortably in the middle of the sky, Haytham decided it was about time to pack it up and head back to eat with Loxas. '*He must be missing me*' he thought with a soft smile.

He stretched the ache from his bones and then headed off back through the busy thoroughfare that had started to coalesce in town.

He hadn't made it too far though before he noticed something, a soft red glow, emanating from one of the darker alleyways.

Noone else in the throng of people seemed to see it but his arcane eye had caught the glimpse easily and now his arcane mind couldn't help but investigate...

The alley itself was surprisingly deep, leading past a series of long, conjoined houses. Still, once he reached the end, he could turn back and see all the people walking by and presumably they could see into the alleyway too.

A fact that had only come to forefront of his mind when knelt down to poke at the glint of a small ruby down amongst the cobbles.

For it was no gemstone – as Haytham's skin made contact with the colour, up floated the body of Archdaemon Loxas. He floated up through the stone of the floor as if it were made of water until his whole form, wearing only those torn trousers, was stood above the warlock.

"Hello, my love. What brings you here?" the daemon teased.

After breaking from his surprise, Haytham squirmed around to try and block the view of his large, red boyfriend but he was just too small to completely cover him.

"You aren't meant to leave the shop!" he hissed, "what are you doing here, people generally don't like daemons, y'know?"

"I'm aware." Annoyed by the warlock's fidgeting, Loxas grabbed both his partner's hands and pulled them up above his head to pin him against the wall. He held them there with just his left forearm so that his right hand was free to pull the defenceless man's chin to look up at him. "Hey, give it a rest. I'm here to ask what's been up with you lately?"

"Well, can we talk about it back home," he grunted, still trying to wriggle free.

"So there is a problem."

"NO, I just..." he was trying to think of some excuse or other when Loxas finally rolled his eyes and lifted his hand up to cover Haytham's mouth.

"Now listen. You're going to tell me what's been bothering you these past few days. If you don't," he lifted his knee to grind against the human's crotch, "then I'm going to start having some fun, hm?"

Haytham's eyes went wide. He shook his head desperately but he was nowhere near strong enough to break from Loxas' pin.

The daemon then removed his free hand from his partner's mouth and slowly slid it down his chest towards the strings of his breeches. Despite the protests he continued to tug and untie until at last they fell to his ankles, bearing his hardness to the chill air.

It wasn't until then that Haytham realised people could see.

No, not 'could.' People are seeing.

His eyes kept darting between his captor – fondling him and making him moan – and the passersby who kept peering down the alley and looking directly at the pair. Tears brimmed in his eyes as he did his best to try and cross his legs and cover his humiliation.

Loxas' own large, hairy thighs stood strongly between him though, forcing him to be exposed to the world.

"The sooner you confess, the sooner I'll let you go, handsome," he teased. He had started pumping Haytham's cock now and causing him to leak all over the muscles of his daemonic leg.

It was as pleasurable as always but this time too shameful. And that made it worse – each eye on his pathetic, whimpering body made another knot of humiliation in his stomach.

"I- I don't want to talk about it," he groaned out, still focused on escaping the grip. "Lo- Loxas plea- PLEASE!" His voice ended up going a volume too loud as he finally spurted all over the midnight hair of the daemon's lower body.

Loxas just tutted at that, "awe, we're not finished yet." He continued to jerk the intensely sensitive dick.

Haytham's squirming turned into thrashing as a sudden unbearable overstimulation overcame his groin.

"No, NO it hurts, fucking, fuck you, LOXAS!" he continued to beg but as long as a confession wasn't leaving his lips the torture continued.

It didn't stop when Haytham squirted all up the daemon's chest; adding to his shame. It didn't stop even when multiple groups of people paused at the end of the alley to watch. Some laughed, some were disgusted; all made him feel embarrassed.

But the worst of all was that it was arousing him. He was a mage and so he knew that Loxas had employed no magic to keep him hard. His weary, oversensitive cock was just loving being used as a torture device. It loved that it no longer belonged to the body it was attached to but instead to the wicked daemon using it to divine information.

After realising this torment would never end, that his dick would continue to contort his body in wave after wave of shocking stimulation, Haytham at last confessed.

"I met an angel! I saw an angel... and it scared me..."

Loxas started being gentle then. He was surprised to hear that this was the secret but at least their heaven conversation had context now.

He let Haytham free and then knelt down to put his clothes back on. When he stood back up, Haytham had crossed his arms and was unable to look him in the eyes. He was sweaty from the exertion but he still leant slightly into the comfort and warmth of the daemon's body.

Loxas also didn't push anymore. He let the air pass over them for a while until his partner was ready to talk.

"I found this," he started by pulling the chunk of the mould shelf from his coat pocket and presenting it to Loxas.

Immediately the daemon understood. "Oh."

"What? What!" Haytham turned to look Loxas in the face again, his expression vulnerable. "You know what this is, don't you?"

He nodded. "It's blight." He put a hand softly on Haytham's forearm to push it away from himself. "And you shouldn't be touching it... I shouldn't even touch it."

"That angel... he was scared of it too."

The daemon spat on the ground, "I'm sure the fucker was. Which of the winged bastards was it?"

"I didn't get a name," Haytham tried his best to explain, "he was blond. Brown eyes, a toga. Taller than me but shorter than you."

"A short angel? Oh *of course* it's him."

"Who?" but Loxas was already moving on. He had closed his eyes, wrapped one arm around his boyfriend, and put one hand forwards. In front of them opened a flaming vortex. Inside the swirling heat was a distorted vision of some outdoor location that Haytham could swear he sort of recognised.

He braced himself to be carried through by Loxas but there was apparently one last thing before they departed.

The daemon cleared his throat. "I, uhm, hope you're not too angry about... you know."

Haytham went red and broke their eye contact again. "Actually it was kind of hot," he mumbled.

A pointed, black finger nail twisted his chin to make him look back at those snake-like daemon eyes. The two stared at each other before pulling into a sweet, mutual kiss. It wasn't hard or hot or heavy like their normal physical exchanges. It was loving.

When they parted - a fragile glimmer of saliva lingering between their soft lips – the daemon grinned.

"Summoning daemons is all the rage these days. You up to summoning an angel?"

Haytham smiled. "It's a date."

# VII

"His name is Taniel."

Loxas answered Haytham's asked question before doing the last thing he expected him to: the daemon got onto his knees and prayed.

The door he had opened in the alleyway took them to a nearby hill in a field about an hour out of town. Haytham recognised the southern edge of the forest nearby but otherwise it was blue skies and green fields.

"Doesn't that hurt?" the human asked.

He saw Loxas' mouth turn up into a smirk, "not me it doesn't."

"And why are we here? Surely a church would be better?"

Loxas shook his head. "High up places are better."

"I think those stories tend to be set on mountains though not... clods."

Loxas ignored him, "it's like how daemons are summoned in lower places like caves," he chuckled, "or cellars."

Haytham bit back his own smile.

As he waited for Loxas' prayers to be answered, he decided to enjoy the serenity of the moment: he walked over to be next to him and ran his fingers through his pitch hair. It was a moment of intimacy in slightly warming midday sun.

Eventually he started to notice the faint clouds above them beginning to part. A stray beam of sunlight flashed across his eyes making him blink and turn away for a moment. When he looked back up he saw the same man as before – the angel Taniel who had inquired about the blight.

He was not quite as angelic now though as he was coughing and pounding at his chest with a fist.

"You *hack* bloody daemons," he spat, choking up embers of fire and specks of yellow sulphur. "You know fully well that you can just speak to us... by... oh," the angel recognised who summoned him.

"Now what do we have here?"

"Long time no see *Taniel*." He pronounced the angel's name the same way as 'Daniel' just to wind that little eye twitch out of him.

"You look different from before?" Haytham pointed out, walking forward to stand next to Loxas. Taniel now had two large, feathered wings sprouting from his back and a glowing halo floating above his golden hair.

He moved a pointing finger between the two other men, "hold on. You... and you? Now, no wonder the blight's been going around."

Haytham looked at Loxas, "so how do you two know each other?"

Loxas didn't look back, he only glared at Taniel. "When I was alive I was a soldier in the greatest empire the world had ever seen. Unfortunately, my emperor hadn't started to believe in God yet so when we attacked a town with His blessing we ended being smote," he held his hand out to the angel before them, "by one of the Lord's protectors."

Taniel made a face of disgust, "you should have been of the faith then."

"You mean I should have been born later! My empire did turn to faith in another hundred years, I was just unfortunate enough to be born under a ruler who didn't believe. But if I had done the exact same things in a life lived a century in the future I would have gone to heaven. Where's the justice in that – that my fate was decided by another man's beliefs?"

"Oh you had beliefs," the angel came in close to Loxas, "you could have chosen a different life, you could have chosen to lay down your weapons rather than fight for a vindictive leader!"

"Words of the privileged," hissed the daemon.

"Please, alright, we can sort this out later!" Haytham interrupted them before a fight broke out, "we need to worry about this right now." He pulled the mushroom out once more. Loxas took a simple step away from it.

Taniel yelped. He lurched back and waved a hand in Haytham's direction. The orange fungus he was holding evaporated into a golden dust that blew away with the wind.

"Watch it!" snarled Loxas. He stepped in front of his boyfriend protectively. Suddenly, bat-like wings of midnight leather were protruding from his back, just as big as the angel's wings. The horns on his head grew too, curling like a ram's.

Taniel was not cowed though. He looked with scrutiny at the pair before gasping as he came to a realisation.

"No, there's no way..." the angel muttered. In one, swift, powerful movement he stretched his arms straight out to the side. As the action finished, the three men suddenly found themselves standing on a field of stars amongst the night sky.

"Woah, woah," Haytham nearly fell over, the vertigo inducing imbalance. Loxas steadied him and explained that they were on the astral plane now.

"But why?" he said turning to Taniel.

"Because I had to be sure... and there it is. Right before my eyes but still hard to believe."

Haytham looked down at his chest to see exactly what the angel was talking about and saw that here his soul was on display. It was whisps of deep blue that were being pulled to the side. He followed the wavering trail all the way to where it met with the crimson reds of Loxas' soul in a purple galaxy that spiralled between them.

"Our love," he whispered, astonished to witness its beauty.

"Abomination," groaned Taniel.

The pair turned to look back at him and saw that his arms were moving again. As they travelled, a bow appeared from the stars themselves, forming and solidifying as he assumed the position of aiming a celestial arrow at their merged souls.

"Don't you dare," Haytham growled. He moved to cast a spell, any spell, to beat this angel down but he was pushed simply aside by the daemon who planned to do the same thing.

Loxas raised his own arm, just the one, in an arc of fire that ended in a crossbow flourishing between his fingers.

"You really need to watch where you point that thing," he warned Taniel.

The two stared each other down for a long moment of thick tension. Eventually Haytham broke the stalemate by walking to stand next to his boyfriend and talking sternly.

"Now tell me, at last, what this whole blight thing is about."

"Oh, your lover didn't explain?"

Loxas continued to glare at Taniel silently.

"Funnily enough I'm asking you." Haytham would definitely bring it up with the daemon later but he had to have his back in front of the angel.

"Blight is a plague on the land. Sure it's edible, delicious even! But that's only to make it so easy to attach onto hosts. It starts in thick patches of black mould where it waits for living beings to come and touch it, to graze against it so that the spores can take them over. It will be slow for you as patient zero but soon it will evolve to be faster, more efficient. Buildings, nature, animals and men will turn black with the rot that the fungus will nurture across the world."

Even Loxas looked scared as the angel's speech spurred fires in the irises of his heavenly eyes.

"W-why?" Haytham asked, "how could this happen?"

"BEACAUSE OF *YOU*!" Taniel seethed. "'Oh, where did the evil, wicked, hellish blight come from?' asks the WARLOCK who bound his soul to a DEVIL."

"He's got quite a fair point there," Loxas conceded.

"No he doesn't!" Haytham said desperately, "I didn't do anything wrong I just- just wanted love, for goodness sakes! And when I couldn't find it in humans I found it in a daemon. Is that so bad?"

He snuggled to the side of Loxas and smiled. He too tried to appeal to the angel's better nature by wrapping his free arm around Haytham's shoulders.

"Hey, I'm not the authority on this," the angel said coldly. "If the Lord thought it appropriate to blight the lands where sinners dwell, who am I to judge him?"

Loxas sneered, "what was that you said before about not fighting for a vindictive leader?"

Taniel was just exasperated. "You know he doesn't love you, right?"

"Of course he do-" Haytham was about to object but the angel held his hand up to him.

"Not you! You," he pointed to Loxas. The human started to realise by then that he was never really considered a valuable part of this conversation between two mythical beings.

"You know that human's love isn't real. On his terms he's just a desperate guy looking for a sad rebound. On your terms he's too smitten by whatever little contract you manipulated him into signing."

"I didn't-"

"I'll be back," Taniel said stoically, not letting the daemon continue to shout. He started to fade, his body glinting away into the stars, "and when I am, I'll bring hordes to wipe this relationship away so that maybe the people of the town can be spared the consequences of your actions."

"The consequences of your God's decisions you mean!" Haytham tried to accuse, although it fell on no ears. For Taniel had faded and with him went the astral plane, depositing the two partners back on that hilltop in the field.

He looked over to Loxas right away to see his eyes slightly sullen. "Are you alright?"

Loxas pulled him into a tight hug. "Of course. I have you." As Haytham hugged back, and the two enjoyed the embrace, Loxas could still hear the angel's words ringing in his head.

'*No*,' he thought. He looked down to the man he loved, that beautiful, precious human, and decided, '*I will prove to everyone that he loves me.*'

# VIII

"I'm getting cold," Haytham complained, "are you nearly done?"

"Oh I was done a while ago." The pair were back in their bedroom where Loxas had insisted on inspecting his boyfriend for any traces of the blight. "I just enjoyed looking," he planted a soft kiss on Haytham's exposed butt that made him yelp. The man had stripped so that Loxas could be completely sure that there were no patches of mould or sprouting shelves. To both their reliefs he was completely clear.

Haytham sat down on the bed, not bothering to dress again. "Do you think that means its growing inside me?"

"Err," Loxas shrugged, "can you feel anything?"

Haytham shook his head. "I have had a bigger appetite recently, though. Maybe that's something to do with it."

"I've only seen bits about a blighting before. I've certainly never seen it take a living host. We'll just have to see," he frowned. He was worried for his love and, based on his own firsthand experience, was very worried that he'd get to hell sooner rather than later.

At least they'd be together down there.

"You know," the tired warlock said, "it's you who's starting to look a bit dour this time." It was only early afternoon but the eventful day had taken it out of him.

Loxas just shrugged, "I think I need something from you."

"Hm?"

"I'm just a bit bugged." He sat down next to his boyfriend, "about what Taniel said about us."

"The love thing?" he asked, an eyebrow raised, "because honestly what would that loser know about love?"

"He was a human once too."

"From what I heard, that was a very long time ago."

"Hm," Loxas agreed, "I do wonder if any of that humanity is left in him."

He felt uncomfortable then as Haytham proceeded to look him up and down. Not hungrily like he normally did but rather curiously. The pair didn't acknowledge it but it was clear he had wondered the same thing about Loxas.

"That's it," the daemon huffed. He stood up, held his hand open and spawned another gateway. "I'm too insecure for this."

"Wait, where are you going?"

"We're going into town. I'm going to rub that snarky angel's expression from my mind."

He grabbed Haytham by the wrist and pulled him to stand up. He ignored the rapid pointing out of the fact that he was naked and simply thrusted him forward and through the spiral of orange flames.

He followed with just a moment's hesitation to calm himself down.

Once through, Haytham had immediately clung to him, trying to hide his nakedness from the large amount of people still out in public. People had stopped to wonder what was going on with the naked weirdo of course but the real crowd had come to gather once he was joined by the daemon.

Loxas didn't move to cover him though.

In fact, he grabbed his boyfriend by the shoulders and turned him around to face the crowd so that everybody could see him. Fascination and disgust made people stare intently at the scene.

"Stop it, stop that!" Haytham tried to get out Loxas' grip. He ended up losing his balance though as his crossed legs, that were trying to cover his shame, caused him to trip over himself. When he was on his knees he had tried to curl up to shroud his form but the daemon was quicker. He pushed roughly at the warlock's back making him fall forward onto his hands and knees.

"Not in public, Loxas please!" he begged as he suddenly felt something warm and hard pressing between his buttocks. The daemon, now nude as well, had gotten on to one knee so that he could slide into the back of the naked man before him.

"Remember what we agreed my love. *Whenever. Wherever.*"

"Bu- but why! I know you're not fussed about this!" His words ended up being cut off by a strangled grunt. Haytham had never bottomed before so the sudden feeling of being filled up had taken over his senses. Yes, the daemon had played with the man's sensitive hole before but it had never been more than his tail that invaded the area.

Now his slick, girthy, cock was pushing as far inside as it would go despite all complaints.

Even Haytham's words had just become pathetic groans as his shaking arms were barely strong enough to hold himself up never mind start resisting.

The heart of his shame was that not only were masses of people just watching in surprise, none of them could even help him if they wanted to.

At some point in the act a man who was watching tried to step in, to push Loxas off. All he got was a burned and blistered hand after making contact with his red skin.

His last defiance was his continued attempt to curl up and hide himself, but once more the much stronger legs of the daemon continued to force Haytham's open.

Soon his tail moved to wrap around his shaft this time – another first in their sessions – as it wound tightly upwards. The tip of the tail rested firmly underneath the tip of Haytham's dick. That was the kicker that turned any waves of pain or discomfort into bolts of pleasure.

The underneath was the sensitive spot on his cock and each time Loxas thrust into him and pushed his hips forward Haytham's head would end up rubbing firmly, in just the right spot, against the heat of the tail.

"Oh Godddd, GOD," he shouted the first time it happened. That was all it took to melt his mind and send his hips into autopilot as they moved forward in a desperate search for that surge of ecstasy again. And even that was merely the opening of the floodgates.

The pleasure had loosened his body up majorly. The discomfort in his rear was turning into another source of those divine waves and now Haytham's body existed to do nought but seek them out.

He moved back hungrily to feel Loxas' cock hit his prostate with warm force and then forward again to overwhelm his dick with the grinding against that luscious tail.

By this point though the city guards had arrived at last. "We're here to help you sir!" one of them declared. They had mail on wrapped in golden tunics. In their hands they both held sharp, gilded spears that they pointed at the daemon.

"NO! No, I want this," he explained. The words fell out of his lolling mouth along with his tongue as he panted like a dog. "I need this!"

Loxas pulled him up then, wrapping his arms around his torso, and held him close to his body. Their slick sweat filled the air with musk and sex as the pair locked eyes. Loxas whispered huskily in his ear, "tell them, baby."

"Fuck, I love this man!" he declared. "I love the Archdaemon Loxas. He's mine!" as he said this he forwent any humiliation. He spread his legs wide open and let everyone bear witness to their intermingling bodies as they fucked like animals.

The two guards didn't know what to do. They just looked at each other, shocked, until one finally had to step away from the shooting ropes of thick semen.

Haytham spurted further than before, his seed feeding the hungry cobbles of Havendon. Loxas finished at the same time and everyone could see his seed overfilling and leaking heavily out from underneath the human.

"Come on, my love," Haytham commanded, brushing a tender hand across the daemon's cheek, "let's go home for another round."

The daemon grinned a wide, spiky grin. "Yes, my warlock master."

The two disappeared in a cloud of grey smoke leaving behind half of Dunmere with a whole new perspective on their resident magician.

# IX

Haytham had been terrified of going back into town after that day. The solution, fortunately, presented itself when the town instead came to him.

In fact it was the very next afternoon when he heard the unexpected sound of his shop's doorbell.

He had been laying bed with Loxas and letting their cuddling wash away any anxieties he had about the reception to their lovemaking in town when it went off.

He ended up cursing a lot as he hopped out of his bed and rushed to messily dress.

"Your coat, Haythe," the daemon reminded him while not deigning to get up and help.

"Yeah, ta," he thanked as he wrapped the blue clothing around him and rushed into the front.

He was especially surprised to find that this customer was an older man and one he recognised no less as a neighbour from just up the street.

"No, no I'm here! How can I help," he said breathlessly while catching the man about to leave.

He got a grumble in response, "playing with your pet, were you?"

Haytham went red. He had realised that this wasn't just any neighbour either, this was one of the people he had asked if there was any mould in their homes after clearing the initial bout.

"Are you here about the strange growth I asked after?"

The man held his nose up, "I am actually... I think I need a professional to remove it."

Haytham nodded and grabbed his key from under the desk ready to go out. He was about to sneak off to say goodbye to Loxas when he smiled and thought to shout instead, "I'm heading out for work! Miss you!"

A deep, "kay!" resounded back and the warlock felt great warmth about their newfound openness.

It plastered a smile on his face that lasted all the way until he got to the kitchen of the old man's bungalow. What he saw there was more than enough to ruin his cheery attitude.

"You, uh, haven't touched it have you?" he asked his client.

"God, no," he rasped in response.

But Haytham couldn't help but doubt as the entirety of three sides of the kitchen wall were covered in the sprouting mould. The shelves of fungus had even grown through some of the cupboards, shattering and splintering the wood open.

It was hard to discern any appliances, cutlery or dishes beneath it all as well. It was just a lump of the blight with vague outlines of furniture that might lie underneath. At the edge of the growth was that telltale sign of consuming black and grey. It folded around the corners where the walls met the floor and ceiling and was starting to creep towards the kitchen door as well.

The next thing Haytham doubted was that the old man had told the truth all those days ago when he inquired after any abnormalities. The woman across the street had claimed hers came overnight but this kitchen was another degree above that. It had to have been festering for a while now.

He even nearly brought it up before deciding that all that mattered was that he had come now rather than never.

So the warlock stretched his neck and flexed his arms before taking in a very deep breath. He only managed to get about a fifth of the blight with that one spell however and had to exert himself heavily to finish the job. By the end of it, once all the mushrooms were burnt away to reveal the cracked room beneath, he was sweating a lot. By even the third casting of the spell he had had to take his coat off and really start warming up his muscles to cope with the exertion of such a large scale controlled fire.

He was extremely grateful that after everything the old man had brought him a mug of water to cool off. He drank it gratuitously, happy that half of it poured down his chin.

The last, and somehow hardest, part of the job was to take his payment. He held out his hand and the old man released his owed silver.

"Thank you. I'm glad you came to me while this was still somewhat manageable."

The customer huffed. "Yeah, yeah."

"Can I ask what changed your mind?"

"Well we thought you were a scammer, all truth be told."

"We?"

"Everyone in Dunmere, really. Can you blame us! You move into the abandoned house by the woods and try to sell us amulets and potions. It wasn't until what we saw yesterday, ahem, that we realised you were the real deal. Not just some peddler of tat but a genuine soothsayer."

"I'm not a soothsayer."

"Be what you will son, if you can do real magic, magic that helps people... well we'll be much obliged."

Haytham smiled. He nearly cried, even, but held it back as there's nothing more rude than being so emotional in someone else's home.

He thanked the man for his patronage and his kind words and then started on his way back home.

He had vigour now though. A verve to cast and help. He decided that he would not go back to the shop until he had knocked on the doors of every house along the street.

And he was glad he did, however much it exhausted him. For three more people had been reluctant to share the fact that they too were suffering from the blight in their houses.

He helped them though and despite the toll it took on him he had earned more money in two hours than he had in the past year.

When he finally finished and got back home and collapsed on the bed he proudly showed off his coin purse to Loxas.

And the daemon was impressed, "wanna celebrate?" he asked immediately, ruining the mood by running a finger up the sweat-ridden thigh of his boyfriend.

Haytham swatted him away. "God, not now, I'm knackered."

"Alright, alright," Loxas bent down and planted a soft kiss on his forehead, "I'll get some food ready for us."

"Mmm," the tired warlock groaned in agreement.

As Loxas walked away Haytham thought to himself *'you could have if you wanted to though.'* And then as he pondered on that sentiment and the fact that he really, genuinely was not in the mood he came across a new thought. *'It wouldn't make him a very good boyfriend though... It's a contradiction in our contract. Fucking me when he wants would make him a bad boyfriend so he can't do both. Seeing as he has only ever been a good boyfriend then that means he has only ever fucked me when... I... actually wanted him too.'*

Haytham bolted to sit up with his realisation. He saw Loxas stood leaning against the doorway and smirking. "You finally figured it out, eh?"

"Why would you sign on if you knew?"

"I still have a human soul deep inside."

Haytham frowned, "you just wanted passageway from hell, did you?"

Loxas shook his head, "that's not what I meant." He walked over and tilted Haytham's chin up gently to look him in the eyes. "There are more than enough ways I coulda escaped that hole. Hell,

I didn't even want anything lame like a man who loved me. What I was looking for," he let his hand fall from Haytham as he suddenly became a slight bit shy, "I wanted someone that was worth loving. Living in hell you see the real brunt of mankind's souls. I never wanted to leave because the more you learn about human nature the less you can tell the difference between hell and earth. But then I saw that cute mage, so exhausted with men but still refusing to give up on love that he even looked to summoning daemons to find it. I just couldn't resist. I felt I needed to wrap my arms around him, to show him the love he needed. And look at you now! You found your treasure and you only let it grow you! You're amazing Haytham Rayne. I love you."

The human finally let those tears hiding behind his eyes fall down his cheeks.

He moved carefully to wrap his hand into Loxas' hair – scared he might just disappear if he acted too eagerly – and pulled him down to bump their two foreheads together. They sat there in a romantic silence, their souls doing all the talking, until at last the warlock was able to speak without sobbing:

"I love you too."

# X

Their integration into the borough ecosystem only seemed to deepen from then on.

There was never a shortage of blight cases to deal with so Haytham was always out of the house in the day time dealing with new sprouts of fungi shelves.

It was only a matter of days as well before someone came into his shop and noticed that he had wares and services other than just the purification.

Before he knew it, there were talismans, runestones, crystals and tags all flying off the shelves. His cellar was becoming stocked with inventory and with all the heavy spellcasting work he had noticed his magic become stronger tenfold.

After all that training a kitchen overrun by blight was just a matter of one small breath in – no sweat.

That did come with the caveat of more work, however. More houses and more people were witnessing cases of the mould. And not only was it starting to reappear in the same houses it already had but people had started seeing it on the pavement, across the city walls and throughout the woods.

Questions were soon starting to be asked after that. Before it was just a mild inconvenience but now it was a question of a threat against the fields. What if it got to the grain and the whole batch had to burn? What if the livestock became infested?

Thankfully, no living creature had been seen getting affected by it yet – only their creations all crumbling around them. But the whispers in the streets were that it's only a matter of time.

The largest purveyor of this wicked gossip was the church. At last, someone had put together that the blight had appeared around the same time that Haytham had started being happier and outgoing which was quickly accredited to his new daemonic lover.

What was once simply a topic of non-discussion was soon spiralling into protests about unnatural relationships.

Just like that, something that everyone had been completely unbothered with before had suddenly turned controversial.

And the church's nasty rumours only continued to draw larger and larger crowds to its side as people became sicker and sicker of the spreading blight.

One of the positives however was that Haytham now had a lot of cash.

So much that Loxas had an idea one day...

He walked into the bedroom that night with his exhausted boyfriend and made a suggestion.

"Have you ever thought about leaving Dunmere?"

It was a suggestion that genuinely confused the warlock. "Why would we leave?"

"With everything going on surely you must be getting tired of it all?"

Haytham did consider that. He had gotten really sick one evening from mana poisoning – if Loxas hadn't used his powers to feed on the excess magic it could have become really serious. But he had only gotten sick from all the casting!

"No, no. It's worth it, it's good work. Besides, someone has to deal with this curse."

"It might come with us if we leave?" he guessed.

"You do know that the blight isn't actually our fault?"

"Yes. *Do you?*"

"What's that supposed to mean?"

Loxas sat down and pulled Haytham's head to rest on his shoulder. He could feel the tenseness in the human's body.

"It just means that you don't have to be the one to deal with it. Hell, it's the God of those bible bashers that put it here, they should be clearing it up!"

"But they won't," Haytham sighed. "I-"

"*Have the ability to clear it so therefore the responsibility,*" Loxas mocked, "I know. You say it every time I have to massage the kinks out of your sore, aching, wounded, torn-"

"Yes, alright!"

"-Body."

Neither had anything to add to that. They just continued to sit in silence in each other's company, Loxas' head now resting atop Haytham's.

There was no animosity in the air; just a frustration that neither knew how to quell.

In the end their argument went unresolved as they simply made a slow move into the covers of their bed. They hugged tightly and let their confusions about their situation melt away in the embrace as they fell into a comfortable sleep.

It was their matter of waking that not only broke this comfort however but also provided them with their definitive response to the earlier predicament.

For Haytham woke to the sounds of shouting.

Of Loxas shouting.

"Huh, what's going on?" He stumbled up, panicking and getting tangled in the sheets with his sleep weary vision. In the next moment, he had been dragged to his feet out of the bed by two large, scary men.

"Get off... fucking, fuck off!" he thrashed against their grip on him, panicking about the fact that there were three spears plunged deep into the chest of his shocked boyfriend.

All it took was as moment of clarity to remember what he could do.

The warlock breathed in hard and deep and tight; blue will-o-the-whisps appeared around his head that shot in darting arrow-like shots at his captors. They burned their exposed skin and dented their armour as they swirled around them in a sharp storm of icy cuts until finally they retreated from the room.

The daemon handled the three by him. When he saw that Haytham was safe he finally worried about himself by shrugging off the three impaling wounds.

"Really guys? No rosemary, no salt, no silver? This isn't even ash wood, for goodness sakes." As he stood up, his chest healed rapidly and pushed the weapons out to clatter on the floor.

Between this sight and witnessing the attack on their fellow soldiers, the final three men fled as well.

"They're still outside," Haytham commented, peering out the window. "A whole host of them."

"Who were they?"

"Reactionaries," Haytham scoffed, spying the local bishops at the head of the surrounding army.

He turned then to look at his boyfriend and frown, "I think it's time for me to accept that you were right... we should go. Let them deal with the blight if they're so insistent."

But Loxas found no satisfaction in that. He may have leapt with joy to hear that not hours ago but seeing Haytham give up broke his heart.

"Before we resort to that," he put a hand on the human's shoulder and tried his best to smile, "you should appeal to your community first."

Haytham smiled wearily back. He put a hand atop Loxas' and nodded, "our community."

When they finally went outside though they saw twenty-three of those armoured guards surrounding the building – the other two injured ones clearly off licking their wounds.

Loxas was stood in the doorway, watching vigilantly. He also had a simple bag packed with all their money, some clothes and food ready in case they had to go.

Haytham was the one who walked out to beg to the kindness of his people.

He tried to start talking, just in the general direction of the ringleaders, but the head of this guard unit spoke over him in a loud and deep voice.

"Haytham Rayne, warlock, you are sentenced to be arrested by royal decree for the crimes of devilist fraternity and spreading infernal disease."

"It's not a disease!" he shouted back.

One of the old, wobbling priests spoke up, "it is a disease on the land!" he accused and some of his nearby sycophants raised shouts of "here, here!"

It was clear to him then that there was nowhere in these people's black hearts for appeal.

So he turned to his townsmen.

Most seemed like they didn't want to be there though, like they too had been dragged from their beds and would rather have it end quickly than make the effort to fight it.

Scouring for people to implore he found the old man, his second blight client, and smiled.

"Tell them, please, that this is a mistake. I'm here to help!"

He tried other begs across many words but the old man ignored them all. He simply stared forwards looking with hollow eyes right through him.

His last resort, he felt, was his very first client. She was there, thankfully, the old woman who came to his door before he was even renowned.

"Please," is all he said to her, his voice falling flat.

She walked up to him and put a hand on his cheek. "Maybe it's for the best, deary. Maybe they can fix you."

The word hit him like a lash.

He wanted to shout in the faces of each and every person here that he was not broken; louder and louder until the cry deafened them all.

Instead he just turned to Loxas, his eyes speaking a thousand words.

He was ready to leave Dunmere now.

The daemon walked forward out of the door frame. The guards reacted swiftly, moving inwards in formation towards the warlock. Loxas was quicker though and he ran to drag Haytham through a swirling vortex of fire that took them out of harm's way.

"It's okay, we're okay now," the daemon did his best to soothe his boyfriend as the two appeared in the middle of large, open field. It wasn't too far away but it was good enough to keep them safe for now. Haytham and Loxas continued to embrace for what felt like forever as they slowly began to accept what had happened.

They were not given too long to process it all though as Haytham noticed something high up in the clouds when he looked over his partner's shoulders.

"I don't think we can celebrate yet," he said morosely. "There's still one more sanctimonious bastard we need to deal with."

For the clouds above them were parting to allow the descent of angels.

# XI

It was not just Taniel this time but him alongside a whole host of cherubim.

Creepy angels with child-like visages that bordered on the uncanny.

Taniel himself was at the head of their descent, his arms spread in faux benevolence.

"Be not afraid."

"Be not an arsehole," Loxas replied, his arms crossed. "What do you want, archangel?"

"I warned you that I would be back to put an end to this farce. Seeing as you resisted the Lord's champions-"

"His police," Haytham corrected.

"It appears that I have to end this abomination where it stands."

He wasted no time in attacking – in going for the kill. While hordes of cherubim swept down to swarm over the warlock, Taniel himself had plucked a beam of sunlight to turn it into a golden rapier. He moved in to rapidly sting and slice at the daemon.

The couple struggled to defend themselves at first.

Loxas sprouted great walls of flame to devour his foe but the angel possessed a deftness that defied overwhelming hellfire.

Haytham could keep shooting spiked flames to take out chunks of the attacking horde but they seemed to refill their ranks whenever he stopped to breathe in again.

It wasn't until they came back to back that their confidences returned.

They switched places, switched foes, on the spot and soon started to lead the attacking.

Great licks of hot flame erupted from the floor to envelop the swathes of cherubim and incinerate their forms.

For Haytham it was as simple as a binding spell. From the ground in front of him shot four metal bands with chains dangling from them. Each band snatched around the wrists and ankles of Taniel where the chains grew suddenly taut.

He was pulled down to the ground where he was locked in place on his hands and knees unable to do anything but squirm.

He did have power to escape still; his body started to flicker out of the material plane as his skin turned transparent and his form phased through its bindings.

Haytham simply strode over, unsheathed his silver athame and made one swift, decisive swipe.

In a glinting arc, he cut both the wings off Taniel's back.

The angel let out a deep, throaty scream as he fell back to his hands and knees. His body became material again as he lost his last method of escape.

"You monsters!" he shouted a raw shout. "I'll fucking kill you both, I fucking swear it, FUCK!" Golden ichor wept from the two stubby wounds on his shoulder blades.

Loxas appeared to like what he saw. "So what do we do with him now?" he asked, recovering his breath from their battle.

"YOU WILL LET ME GO AND ANSWER TO GOD!" he screeched.

"Shut him up," Haytham groaned.

"How?"

The warlock was going to suggest something simple like a gag but then he saw the way that Taniel's body was bound and positioned and suddenly a new, hungry thought entered his mind.

"With your cock," he suggested.

"*What*?" Taniel said with dread.

"You heard the pretty man," Loxas shrugged as he tugged his trousers down, "now quiet down."

He shoved his flaccid dick into the mouth of the thrashing angel, filling it with hot, red meat.

"I'm liking this plan of yours, my love. I've always wanted to hate-fuck this guy." As he said that, his dick grew harder and longer causing Taniel to start to choke as he made slow movements in and out.

Haytham was stood at the other end of the angel, enjoying caressing the curve of his arched back. His fingers trailed down to start feeling all over the soft, round ass that was unwillingly protruding.

"Now, mister archangel. Not only did you sentence my man here to eternal torture in hellfire you also came down here today to condemn me to the same fate. Not even to mention your complacency in letting the blight do whatever it's going to do mankind. Are you ready to experience even a fraction of the pain you made us feel? Hm?"

As he talked, he was slowly leaning down towards the angel's ears, his voice getting lower and sharper. What had once been a struggling person in their grasp had now become a shameful man barely able to shake his head in disagreement. It brought a macabre satisfaction to Haytham to see that Taniel was admitting in regret.

"Be a good boy and... try to enjoy it, eh?" Loxas teased, slapping the side of the angels face.

On Haytham's end, he wasted no time in turning up the lower parts of the toga to reveal the nudity underneath. And he had to give it to the angel, he really was a thing of beauty.

The warlock enjoyed a few indulging moments of groping, kissing, spanking and licking at the treasure before him. When he was satisfied, and his cock had reached the height of its impatience, he finally moved to spread open his prize.

"MMPHHFF!" the angel's muffled protests whined out as he experienced sodomy for the first time.

Haytham went in hard and unrelenting, enjoying the feeling of tightness that came from a literally heavenly ass.

Back in the front, Taniel was merely trying to cope with the overwhelming musk that pushed into his nostrils each time the daemon thrusted into his throat. Each time Loxas did, his trail of black pubic hair buried the angel's nose in a sweat that reeked of masculinity.

He tried to block the situation out, mentally pretend it wasn't happening, but soon he started to feel the practiced fucking of the human digging into his special spot. He looked up to see that the two men didn't even care as they were making out above him in sloppy kisses. He was even starting to experience an orgasm that rippled through his body with each violent stab. It even felt good that his mouth was full – it was a warm, grating pain that titillated the nerves inside his throat and turned his body into an orchestra of ecstatic instruments.

And it truly caused him to feel a frustration like no over in his life and afterlife as suddenly his attackers stopped. He hadn't even noticed it as he was too enveloped in his own pleasure but at some point his holes had been filed and left dripping with the thick cum of Haytham and Loxas.

"Wait no, please," he begged, spitting the salty white out of his mouth. "Don't just stop there, have mercy I beg you, mercy!"

Haytham laughed at him. Loxas walked around to stand by his partner, both of them admiring the messy, twitching hole of their third.

"What do you say, babe? Wanna finish milking this cow?" Loxas leant in and grabbed both of Taniel's cheeks, pulling them apart to stick his tongue inside and greedily lick at the bodily fluids inside.

"I suppose we had better," Haytham conceded.

He grabbed the upside down dick of the angel and pumped hard and fast with one hand. With the other, he consistently slapped at the angel balls, mixing his delight with aching.

The two continued to work his lower body like this, out of his vision, leaving him to shudder in the throws of the most humiliatingly shameful orgasm he would ever experience.

He had once been a great man, elevated to paradise. Now he was just an animal to have his seed tortured out of him.

When he was done though – satisfied at last – he uttered one final, pathetic groan.

"Huh?" the human wondered, "what was that?"

"Da- Danazel," he repeated.

"Oh for God's sake," Loxas cursed. He got up to grab their things and try to leave. Haytham was confused but trusted the daemon and went with him into a new spiral of flaming portal. Before they could even touch it however it had been blown out by a golden wind as Taniel repeated his summons in a last, defiant shout.

"DANAZEL!"

"Is that another angel?" Haytham asked nervously.

"He's a fucking seraph," Loxas confirmed as this time the clouds did not just part but instead left the sky completely.

From the sun itself descended a man as tall as a castle.

# XII

He had hair that was pure black but not in the midnight way that Loxas' was. His eyes were a rich, sky blue and his skin a soft, golden porcelain. He wore a toga, although that was a sight much more dignified than the opened one of the still chained Taniel. From his back he sprouted three pairs of wings that rested behind him in a glorious section of six.

The only outlier to a figure like this, one of the few beings that can claim to be close to the image of the Lord, was his face.

It was psychotic; wide-eyed and smiling incessantly.

"What trouble have you gotten yourself into now, brother Taniel?" he asked. When he spoke his voice was perfect. Too perfect. It made Haytham deeply uncomfortable.

"Oh great seraphim-"

"*Seraph,*" he corrected sternly. "Seraphim is plural. But do continue."

Taniel swallowed; his face deeply red from his compromising position. "Could you please free me from these bonds, lord seraph."

"Hm," Danazel considered. "Maybe I will after learning of how you got into them. That seems fair, doesn't it?"

"I was... apprehended while attempting to smite these two."

The two boyfriends had hoped to go unnoticed. Now that the seraph's eyes were on them though they felt a sudden pity towards Taniel.

"Ah yes. The human-daemon soul bond. Might I ask why you were interfering here when the Lord almighty in heaven had already placed a blight around them?"

"Th- they needed to be punished!"

"AND YOU THOUGHT YOU HAD THE RIGHT TO OVVERIDE GOD'S EXISTING PUNISHMENT?" as he shouted in his fury his voice grew distorted and staticky. "Or did you simply want to come up with an excuse to further punish the human that battled you to pissing yourself when he was still alive?"

When Taniel hung his head in shame, too pitiful to acknowledge the astounding truth, Danazel finally deigned to wave his wrist and break the bonds on the archangel. He just sat there, curled up in self-loathing.

"And as for you two," he turned back to the warlock and the daemon. "While the blight was sufficient punishment for your soul bond, it appears that you require further chastisement for the rape of my colleague here."

Haytham snarled, stepping forward and fearlessly standing up to the seraph, "he deserves worse a thousandfold for the torment he put my love through. Actual, literal *hell*," he rasped.

The action and the words galvanised the previously scared Loxas to do the same. He stepped by him and faced his fate with guts. "And to be honest, was kind of begging by the end there."

"ENOUGH OF THE INSOLENCE," his words came out like a sonic boom. "Archdaemon Loxas, lord of men. While I cannot sever two soulmates, I can physically ensure they never see each other again in all eternity."

"*No*," he begged.

"You will be sent back to hell, down to the deepest, darkest, coldest circles this time, where you may never be in the presence of this warlock again.

"NO!" he shouted.

But the noise of his complaint simply faded in echo. He was gone. In a poof of stardust, the daemon left the mortal plane once again.

"L- Loxas," Haytham whimpered, pawing at the air where he once stood.

"As for you, Haytham Rayne-"

"AGH!" the warlock screamed. He pulled his athame out once more, its blade still dripping with ichor, and stabbed rapidly and violently into his own chest again and again and again and again and again.

He killed himself in a vile attempt at slinking into the same pits of the underworld as his lost lover.

"How sad," Danazel commented. He snapped a finger and suddenly the bleeding corpse of Haytham was taking a sharp intake of breath, alive once more.

"Undead, actually," Danazel explained. "Welcome back lord vampyre."

Haytham looked down in horror as his milky white skin was stitching itself back together as if the wounds hadn't been there at all.

"What have you done to me?"

"Well it wouldn't be fair if you just got to reunite that easily now would it? I've transfigured you into an immortal beast of the dark. You are now the vampyre, Haytham Rayne, first of your kind. You will live forever, stitching yourself back together with a soul that cannot leave this realm. You will never see your partner again for not even death is freedom from God's will."

Haytham fell to his knees in despair. He looked down at his hands, gaunt and white and shaking, and started to weep. His first instinct was to try. Surely there was something that could kill him? But as he continued to process his new body, his new soul, he started to feel deep in his invincible bones that there truly was nothing for now but un-life.

"That is that then," Danazel patted himself on the back. He started to rise, satisfied with his work when he heard the chirping of his fellow angel once more.

"Wait, take me with you. I've lost my wings, I need help," groaned Taniel.

"Oh right," Danazel acknowledged, although he didn't stop his ascent. "No."

"No?"

"You are no longer welcome in our hallowed halls. For you are broken. Used. Someone else's toy."

Taniel blubbered out a shocked retort but Danazel was set in climbing upwards until he was nothing but a spec forgotten in the sky.

The only thing that broke him out of his maddening babel was the sudden visceral hissing behind him.

He turned to see steam swirling off of Haytham as the light of the sun burned his skin. He didn't run though. He ate the pain up.

"I WILL KILL YOU DANAZEL," he shrieked. "No. Not even. THAT'S NOT GOOD ENOUGH. Hear me o lord who art in heaven. HEAR ME. I am going destroy your creation piece by piece. Mankind will BURN as long as they worship you, BURN until nothing is left but my empire of the night!" He walked forward then, heading like a slow, marching beast – still burned by the sun – down towards Dunmere. Towards men. Towards the world he would raze just to stoke a fire half as hot as the one burning in his heart for lost love.

To be continued

in book two...

Heavy Mettle: Empire

Coming soon...

# Also by Lewis King

For more info as well as updates about future releases, head to @lewiskingauthor on Instagram, Tik Tok and Twitter.

*"Ancercy is the fatal disease spread to mankind when they sleep with daemons.*

While the south of an otherwise unremarkable kingdom becomes embroiled in an epidemic of this foul affliction, and those within seek the desperate cure, there are those without who are working to hasten the spread of ancercy.

And with the mayor's son starting to be turned away from parlour doors, even the queen has taken time from her daughter's baptism to attend to the matter; a baptism through which the future of this very kingdom will be told in smoke and water.

A future at whim to the designs of witchers and the commands of clergy - a kingdom of ambitious men. But not one made without the decisions of three women in particular: the magister, the whore and the princess... the daughters of God."

Head to phoenixclarke.co.uk for more info or buy now on amazon in paperback, hardback and kindle + KU.